THE ZOMBIE
PHILOSOPHER

A Novella

Richard Wagner

Illustrations by Paul Forney

PAGE PUBLISHING
Conneaut Lake, PA

First originally published by Page Publishing 2022

ISBN 978-1-6624-8259-5 (pbk)
ISBN 978-1-6624-8267-0 (digital)

Printed in the United States of America

To my wife, Andrea, and to the philosopher, David Chalmers, whose *philosopher's zombie* thought experiment inspired some of my own investigations.

CONTENTS

INTRODUCTION

General fiction is pretty much about ways that
people get into problems and screw their lives up.
Science fiction is about everything else.

—Marvin Minsky

I wanted to tell a story of future relationships of people to machines. Such a fiction must be set far enough in the future so that the machines have some genuinely interesting but realistic properties and not so far in the future that magical appearing properties are expected. This is hard science fiction. Nothing here is supernatural or violates known physics. There are no time machines and no faster-than-light spaceships—only real possibilities.

CHAPTER 1

Purchase

You are what you do, not what you say you'll do.
—Carl Jung

The smell of pear blossoms was in the air. Winter was ending. Red buds of new growth were on the branches of the black oaks. It would soon be time to remove the pool cover and put up the tennis net. I walked outdoors from my house in the country to look at the morning sky—bright cerulean with slowly drifting clouds—and picked up a few fallen twigs from the ground. I had a lot to do, and I began to make a mental list of needed actions indoors and out.

There were green buds on the liquidambar trees, and some of last fall's leaves and seedpods were on the ground too. It was time to get ready for spring and summer activities. To help with my chores, I was considering getting a personal robotic assistant. It wasn't so much about the prestige of owning one, as it was the sheer convenience of having one and the added free time it would mean to me.

Back in the house, I made a table of the advantages and disadvantages of obtaining a personal assistant and valet. It would have to be of the male-gender-identifying type because a valet would be expected to assist me in dressing, and a female type might appear unseemly. On the plus side were all the things he could do to save time for me. He could make coffee, answer the door when visitors arrived, accompany me to the store, and carry groceries into the

1

house when we returned. And after some training, he might even go to the store alone and run other errands for me. On the negative side, all I could think of was the initial cost and the space he would take up in the house and car. The cost of the electricity he would consume at his charging station was not a factor due to my extensive photovoltaic rooftop panels. I get a small payment each month from the electric utility.

As I had the money, the decision seemed easy, so I messaged a dealer in town and arranged a meeting to discuss particulars. It would take over an hour to get to the city from my home in the country in my ground car, but my flying car would take less than half an hour, so I scheduled a takeoff for after lunch. Powered by liquid hydrogen, my air car doesn't really cost much to use because I have an electric water hydrolyzer and a cryogenic storage tank in a shed next to the landing pad. I keep the fuel tank topped up so it's always ready to fly. I had named my flying car Maxine, and I called my ground car Davy.

Having preloaded the instructions into the autopilot, I walked out to the landing pad and got into Maxine after lunch.

Maxine said, "I'm fully fueled and ready to go, Mr. Collier. I have your instructions."

Maxine lifted off and flew the two-hundred kilometers in a few minutes, directly into a landing slot in the side of the dealer's building. Maxine shut down her turbines, and I got out and rode the elevator down to the dealer's showroom where he greeted me.

"Welcome, Mr. Collier. I understand that you're interested in a personal assistant. Are you thinking of leasing or buying?"

"I've run the numbers and buying makes more sense in my case," I said.

"An excellent choice. I see you self-identify as male gender, so I assume you will want our male model personal assistant with standard security and valet software packages."

"Yes," I said. "That's right. I've done my research, and that's why I selected your brand, and I think I know the model I want."

"Good, good," he said. "So you know about the multi-petabyte memory capacity and infinite trainability! Excellent."

"There's just one custom addition I would like, if possible," I said.

"Yes, what's that?"

"I would like you to add in some memory filtering software. I don't want him filling up his long-term memory storage with repetitious trivialities. Just add a feature that only transfers from short-term to long-term memory events that have a signifier coefficient above, say, 30 percent. That is, he should remember special instructions and unusual events."

"I think we can do that," the salesman said, "but it might take an extra week or two."

"Fine," I said. "I can wait. Just let me know if it will be longer than that."

I signed some papers, purchased an extended warranty and a two-year renewable service package, and made the account transaction. The salesperson said they would let me know in a week how the special modification was coming and would send the robot to me in a few weeks.

I took my leave, and taking the elevator up to the car park, I got into Maxine, flew home, landed at my pad a short walk from the house, and got out when she opened the passenger door. Then I hooked up the liquid hydrogen refueling hose to keep Maxine ready for a flight.

The next day, the dealer let me know that the software team had said my robot assistant could be ready in two weeks, and they would be more specific as the day approached.

A few days later, I met my friend, Margaret, at a restaurant for dinner and told her about my purchase.

"That's really cool, Edward," she said. "I'll bet he could help you work on your tennis game too."

Margaret has short brown hair and green eyes and is an artist who has a home business making jewelry but, unfortunately, doesn't play tennis.

"I hadn't thought of that," I said. "There are probably a zillion ways he can help me that I haven't thought of. It's going to be fun!

What do you think of ordering this Central Coast Chardonnay to go with our crispy zucchini bruschetta appetizer?"

"That sounds good! I'd like to try it. You must be keeping busy with your software consulting work to be able to buy a personal assistant."

"Work is keeping me busy," I said. "My software design skills are in demand, so I only need to work a couple of hours a day for some extra spending money, which is nice."

Human productivity had increased so much due to technological innovations that poverty had been eradicated a long time ago, and the social safety net had been extended to the point that everyone received a stipend sufficient to live on; nobody had to work unless they wanted to. Politicians had realized that due to accelerating productivity gains from technological innovations, if they didn't sufficiently tax the rich to implement social programs and reduce working hours, soon most people would be unemployed and impoverished. Historians call that period of social progress the *great liberal revolution*.

Our waiter removed our appetizer plates and refilled our wine glasses as we continued our tête-à-tête. Then our entrées arrived, and we tucked in. After we finished, Margaret asked with a mischievous smile and a twinkle in her eye, "Do you want to come to my place for dessert later? We can take my car, and you can send Davy home."

"That will be super," I said.

After I paid the bill, I sent my ground car the nearly five kilometers home. Margaret's car had a front bench seat and a back bench that folded down for extra cargo space if needed. We got in the front, and the car rolled out onto the highway. The car was equipped with seatbelts for those who feel more comfortable wearing them, but younger people today grew up without them. Human driving of cars and trucks was outlawed many years ago. As a result, car accidents have become extremely rare.

I rode with Margaret to her house where we had some cognac to go with dessert. It was delicious. We talked some more, and as it was getting late, Margaret invited me to stay the night.

*   *   *   *   *

In the morning, she scrambled up some eggs with chorizo. "This is good!" I said, and then I smacked myself on the forehead. "Oh gosh, I should have ordered the chef software package! I can still do that, I suppose."

Margaret said, "I checked it out. A chef package isn't offered yet. The development team couldn't decide between French and Italian cooking, so they decided to offer both, and they're still working on it. But I think it will be fun to teach him to cook yourself."

"Yes, I can do that, and it will be fun. Like teaching him to play tennis. For a while, I should be able to win against him, and then he'll have to deliberately tone it down to keep me interested. It's no fun getting beaten all the time."

"And you could teach him chess and enjoy beating him for a while until he learned opening theory the hard way."

"There are all kinds of possibilities," I said. "It won't be long now until he arrives."

I returned to my house in Margaret's car and then sent it back to her, thinking of the prospects for when my personal assistant arrives.

CHAPTER 2

Delivery

A computer would deserve to be called intelligent if it could
deceive a human into believing that it was human.

—Alan Turing

The day of arrival came, and I heard the whining-hissing sound
of the four steerable nozzles of a public flying car as it descended
for a landing on my pad, not far from my own air car. My personal
assistant got out and walked toward the house carrying a package. He
was dressed in the valet outfit that came with the software package:
dark-gray slacks, black shiny shoes, a white shirt with slim dark tie, a
light coat, white fabric gloves, and bowler hat. When he had moved
away from the car a sufficient distance, it took off and flew away. I
greeted him at the front door.

"Welcome to my house," I said. "I am Mr. Collier. Come in.
What shall I call you? And don't say 'Jeeves'!"

"I don't know, sir," he said. "I suppose it is up to you to name
me."

My new assistant was the latest model, and he had lips, tongue,
and vocal cords for speaking, not just a speaker as in some older
models.

"All right, let me think about it a bit," I said, "but if I start calling
you 'hey, you,' step in and suggest a name! What's in the package?"

"This is my charger. It plugs into an electrical outlet and mounts to a wall. When I'm not busy, I can stand against it, and it charges my battery by induction."

"All right, we'll find a good place to put it," I said, "and I've decided on a name for you. I'll call you 'Brent,' if that's all right with you."

"Very good, sir," said Brent, as he stepped into the entry hall, put his hat on the sideboard, put down the package, removed his coat, and hung it in the closet.

The makers of human-form robots had stopped trying to imitate humans too closely long ago. There's a psychological "uncanny valley," which, as the robot form approaches an exact resemblance to humans, would get creepy. Brent was obviously robotic with a metallic outer surface and smooth somewhat-humanlike features. The simple abstract-looking ears had functional lobes with canals feeding into tiny microphones for stereophonic hearing. The eyes were obviously lensed spherical cameras with a humanlike range of motion. The spec sheet said he could also see a limited range of infrared which would come in handy for nighttime security.

"I don't have any pets to take care of. I'll give you a quick tour of the house and show you where I keep the tools so you can install your charger later," I said and led the way through the living room and into the kitchen. "I suppose you'll be needing the house network password."

"No, sir, I already accessed it. Using the device name, plus '1234' is not a secure password, sir. I changed it and updated all your attendant devices too, so we're all in communication now. It's part of the security package you paid for."

"Thanks, I think."

The flying car that delivered my robot valet
ascended from my landing pad.

In the kitchen, Brent said, "You have many fully automated appliances, sir. I know the contents of your fridge, freezer, and pantry without opening them."

I said, "My friend, Margaret, and I talked about how it might be fun to teach you how to cook. What do you think about that?"

"That could indeed be interesting, sir. I'm quite willing to give it a try. Many of the food items in your kitchen stores have suggested recipes attached to them, and I would be happy to build on those. I'm going to need an apron for kitchen work and some rubber gloves for washing up afterward. The gloves can come in handy for other washing chores too. There are some other items I will be needing in the course of my duties, and I can give you a list."

Brent's list appeared on my personal device and included some standard valet items like a silver tray and a clothes whisk. He also wanted a solar umbrella and some smaller items. I authorized him to charge my account within the limit of a reasonable household budget and told him as much, saying, "Go ahead and order the things that you require."

"Thank you, sir."

We went back into the living room, and Brent, noticing my bookcase, said, "I see you are a bibliophile, sir."

"Yes, I read and collect some of the classics. There's nothing like turning a real paper page. Some of these books are quite rare." I walked over to the shelves and showed him the latest addition to my collection, John Steinbeck's *The Acts of King Arthur and His Noble Knights*.

"Now, Brent, let's go out to the backyard, and I will show you some outdoor tasks." We walked out the kitchen door to the side yard and then headed around to the back.

"Tell me, Brent, what else is included in the security package?"

"Sir, I have skills in various empty hand martial arts, I have familiarity with light weapons, and I know some moves to disarm intruders."

"Does that mean you'd be willing to take a bullet for me?"

"Yes, sir, but I hope it would not come to that. I have some skill at de-escalation in case of conflict. But if I misjudge a situation and a firearm should be discharged in my direction, I will continue to operate and defend as I am able. Do not think that I am particularly brave. My hardware can be replaced, and my software and memories are backed up to the corporate cloud, so I am essentially immortal."

"Yes, Brent, I can see that. Your fortitude will bring me confidence in any stressful situation. Here we are at the swimming pool, surrounded by a fence. It's important to keep the gate closed to keep a toddler from wandering in. Are you waterproof enough that you could rescue a child who happens to fall in?"

"I shall endeavor to keep the pool gate closed when adults are not around. I am sufficiently water-resistant to undertake a pool rescue, but I am not warranted for extended or deepwater operations. Wiping down with isopropyl alcohol is recommended after full immersion."

"Very good, Brent," I said. "As you see, I have solar panels on an overhead structure at the far end of the pool to provide shade for my guests who prefer it. There is also a cabinet with a combination lock down there where we can keep a jug of alcohol should you ever need it. Now let's go look at the tennis court." We walked over to the tennis court, which was enclosed in a high fence with green wind cloth and a practice backboard at one end.

"Friends of mine come over to play tennis with me from time to time," I said. "Do you know how to play?"

"I am sorry, sir. I do not have any sports packages installed, but I can learn if you like."

"We'll give it a try some time," I said. "Then you can help me practice my skills."

"Very good, sir," said Brent.

I said, "When I'm alone, I can practice with the backboard. It's an excellent opponent and can return all my shots except for my lobs."

Brent said, "Indeed, sir. The backboard would have to be exceedingly high to return your lobs."

"That was a joke, Brent."

"Yes, sir. Very good, sir."

Just then a squirrel came down from a tree in the yard, ran across the grass, up into another tall tree, and sat on a branch, chattering at us.

Brent asked, "Do you have any idea what the squirrel is saying to us, sir?"

"I think he's telling us not to mess with any of the acorns he has cached in the ground around here, but I don't believe squirrels have symbolic language as we know it."

"Mr. Collier, are there any dangerous animals about that I should know of?"

"Fortunately, we have no poisonous snakes or alligators around here. There are probably some bears and mountain lions in the mountains you see off in the distance there, but they don't come around here. I don't have a fenced yard, but then I don't have any children or pets."

Brent and I walked back into the house.

I asked Brent, "Do you know how to play chess? I could use a practice partner to brush up my skills so that I can impress my friends, Martin and Carl, when either comes over for a game."

"I am sorry, sir. I do not have any board or card game packages installed."

"No worries, I'll teach you," I said. "Maybe I can even beat you a couple of games while you're learning." I pointed out some areas around the house for routine inspection and cleaning. "Later I'll give you a list of routine chores I want you to do for me."

"Very good, sir."

I compiled a list of chores for him and transferred it to him from my personal device.

Then I set up the chessboard, and showed Brent how the pieces move and told him the rules of the game. It turned out that I did not win a single chess game against him. I hadn't discussed opening theory nor how to win with a pawn in the endgame, but his processing is so fast that he can think ten moves ahead in a few minutes. Even with my experience in strategy, he was beating me on tactics.

Later I assisted Brent in installing his charger on a living room wall where he would stand when not busy with chores and at night while I slept. He proved adept at serving meals, cleaning the kitchen, and helping with various chores both inside and outside the house.

CHAPTER 3

Dinner Party

Knowing your own darkness is the best method for dealing
with the darknesses of other people. It would help you to
have a personal insight into the secrets of the human soul.
Otherwise, everything remains a clever intellectual trick,
consisting of empty words and leading to empty talk.

—Carl Jung

Tuesday evenings I go to the chess club in town for a bit of mental
exercise and conversation with my chess friends. I had played in
tournaments when I was younger, and I still enjoyed playing for the
beauty of the game and the friendly competition. I usually play several fifteen-minute games, and the club maintains a ranking system
that is calibrated to the interplanetary chess federation. After a club
game, the winner reports the result to a club officer, and the rankings
are updated instantly. My ranking has stabilized in the upper third of
the club's two dozen or so regular members.

Carl and Martin are two of my friends at the club with whom
I play frequently, and I invited them both to the house the follow-
ing weekend for a small soiree I was throwing for a few friends for
some fun and conversation and to introduce them to Brent. Then
I rode home in Davy, my ground car, replaying a chess game in my
head on the way.

The next afternoon was warm and sunny, so I went for a dip in my pool. I lay in the sun for a while on one of my *chaise longues.* Brent brought me an iced tea on his silver tray.

"Thank you, Brent," I said. "Is it true that a valet will assist his master in dressing too?"

"Indeed, sir, those skills are included in my valet software package. I can select appropriate garments and assist you in putting them on. I even know how to tie a shoelace."

"A what?"

"It's an old-fashioned, stringlike, shoe-fastening device," said Brent.

Brent brought me an iced tea on his silver tray.

"You don't say. Well, I don't have any of those. I'll be in to get dressed in about an hour."

"Very good, sir. If you don't mind, I will bring my umbrella out here and enjoy the solar-charging for a while."

I didn't mind his company. Brent held his umbrella and looked off into the distance while I went back to reading my book. There's nothing like reading old-fashioned style paper pages.

Later Margaret came over to give Brent a cooking lesson and stayed for dinner. She had brought some special ingredients, and we had a real feast. They cooked synthetic crab meat, fresh asparagus, and new potatoes. Brent couldn't taste food, but he learned how to prepare what people like. Brent cleaned up while Margaret and I talked on the couch.

"Brent is a natural in the kitchen," she said, "he's super dexterous, and it's nice that he knows where everything is without looking for it."

"Yes, he seems to learn quite quickly," I said.

Margaret got ready to leave. I walked her out to her car.

"Good night," I said, "see you at the dinner party this weekend."

"Good night," she said, as the car door closed and off she went.

*   *   *   *   *

On the evening of the party, Margaret arrived early bringing an *ikebana* she had made and set it on the dining table as a centerpiece.

"That's lovely," I said, "thank you."

My tennis partner Joe and his girlfriend Angela, a teacher of philosophy at the college in town, came in next. Victoria, a lawyer and my neighbor across the tree-lined road, also attended. Martin and Carl tested their chess skills against Brent, who made his moves on the board between serving drinks and bringing out hors d'oeuvres.

Heavyset Martin said, "Damn, he hardly looked at the board, and he beat me rather easily."

After starting a game with Carl, who is slender, Brent said, "I don't need to be looking at the chessboard while doing my thinking. The board serves as a mental prosthesis to remind human players of the current position, and it lets me know what moves you make. For me, the game is an internal abstraction of piece designations in an eight-by-eight matrix and a numerical evaluation function for positions arrived at by possible moves. I only need to see the opponent's move in real time to know what the current position is."

In the middle game, a piece and a pawn down, Carl resigned the game.

"That's enough for me," he said.

We all sat at the dinner table while Brent served the food and refilled our wine and water glasses.

Margaret said, "It looks like Brent is really working out well for you, Edward."

I said, "Yes, I'm quite pleased with my purchase. The capabilities of these new generation robots are amazing. I'm going to take him with me when I take my next holiday." Brent was removing the empty plates now.

"Do you have any idea where you're going to go?" Margaret asked.

"I've visited every continent in the world now, so I'm thinking that maybe I'll go someplace more exotic like the moon, Mars, or one of the asteroid colonies this time." Brent began serving coffee and dessert and after-dinner drinks for those who wished.

Joe, who had curly blond hair, an infectious smile, and liked to wear shorts all the time, not just when he was playing tennis, asked, "Have you tried playing tennis with Brent yet, Edward?"

"I haven't gotten around to that yet, Joe. I'm going to take him into town and get him fitted for tennis shoes and get him a racket and some shorts and things."

"Sounds good," Joe said. "It will be interesting to see how rapidly he learns the game and how good at it he becomes."

"Indeed," I said. "It should be fun. If he catches on well, we can try doubles with you and Angela."

Joe is a propulsion engineer with an air transport company in the city. He works from home, like me, and likewise flies to the city once a week for in-person meetings. Joe loves to talk about technology, and my friends indulged him over coffee, liqueur, and dessert at the dining table. Margaret asked Joe a question about hydrogen fuel.

Joe explained, "Hydrogen has the highest energy to weight ratio of any fuel, making modern flying cars possible. Over a century ago, before fossil fuels were outlawed, medium chain hydrocarbons were commonly used for aviation propulsion. Those fuels have a hydrogen atom to carbon ratio of about two to one.

"Later, as people realized the importance of climate stability, methane fuel, which has a hydrogen to carbon ratio of four to one, became a technological stepping-stone toward the use of pure cryogenic hydrogen. All the relevant technologies involving cryogenic fuel were tested and perfected using methane."

Margaret asked, "But isn't hydrogen more dangerous than hydrocarbon fuels?"

"I'm glad you asked that, Margaret. That's why aviation couldn't move to cryogenic hydrogen all at once. Methane is safer than hydrogen but more dangerous than the longer chain hydrocarbons. Hydrogen has a much wider range of explosive combinations with air. With cryogenic fuels, there is always some boil-off because there are no perfect thermal insulators.

"Engineers found that using positive ventilation, that is by diluting fuel vapor with enough fan-blown air, the explosion risk could be controlled down to near zero. And that is the technology that makes home-production of cryogenic hydrogen possible today, so anyone who wants one can have a fueled-up and ready-to-fly car at home."

Margaret said, "Thanks, Joe. I like that explanation. I hadn't known about methane being a major step in arriving at modern air transport technology."

We talked some more about local events in town and mutual acquaintances. The community center in town was going to start offering yoga and tai chi classes. The owner of the tennis shop was thinking of retiring. After coffee, my friends departed, and I gave Brent a hand in cleaning up the kitchen before hitting the sack. I went upstairs to my bedroom, and Brent stood watch against his charger in the living room.

*   *   *   *   *

The next morning after my shower, I walked into the kitchen to start breakfast, and just out of curiosity, I asked Brent, "At night, while charging in the dark, what do you think about? Do you sleep or dream? If you don't sleep, do you find it boring?"

Turning on the coffee maker, Brent replied, "I don't sleep or dream as people do, but charging time at night gives me a chance to download software updates and to upload selected memories to long-term cloud storage. I can also put myself into a low-power mode, but I retain observation functions of the household sensor system for security monitoring. I do not experience boredom, sir."

"I see," I said. "It's good to know you're never bored. Let me show you how to cook eggs."

"Very good, sir," said Brent.

I got a small frying pan off the wall and some butter and two eggs from the fridge. Then I put the pan on low heat and put some butter in the pan. "First, I'm going to show you how to crack an egg with one hand." I cracked an egg on the edge of the pan and opened it into the pan. "You see, there is no eggshell in the egg. The shell in my hand goes into the organic recycling. Now you try it."

Brent repeated my motion and said, "Just like in the movie *Sabrina* with Audrey Hepburn."

"How do you know that?" I asked.

"I have Internet access to public domain video and other media," he said, "so I sometimes like to watch classics of cinema."

I said, "That is a good way to learn more about human culture, particularly about how our present state developed. I suppose you have your favorite film genres."

I showed Brent how to fry an egg in the way I like it. "It's important not to scorch the egg, and temperature control is the key. If the egg gets scorched, the hard film has a metallic taste."

Over the next several days, I taught him several more egg breakfast dishes including scrambled, poached, and omelet. After breakfast, we cleaned up the utensils and kitchen and walked back out to the living room.

Brent said, "Mr. Collier, I notice you have a gun on the wall."

Brent was referring to my old-fashioned flintlock musket, a Brown Bess, of the type used by both sides during the war of the American Revolution, complete with bayonet.

I said, "Yes, that flintlock musket is a reproduction, not an antique, which is why it's in such good condition. But you don't have to worry, it's attached securely to the wall with a combination lock, and only I know the combination."

Indeed, the wall rack for the musket had a four-letter multiple-dial combination lock. The possible number of combinations is 26^4 or 456,976. Trying one combination per minute would take ten months to try them all.

I also have some pictures on the wall. One is a reproduction Jackson Pollock drippy style painting. Another is a Willem de Kooning copy. I have enough income for my needs, but I would have to be rich to collect original artworks. There is a saying about art that one should purchase only art that one can live with, and I enjoy the abstract expressionists. There is no public art museum in town, but there is one in the city, and it should be interesting to take Brent there and see what he thinks about the various kinds of art. I will bring it up later and see what he thinks.

CHAPTER 4

Shopping

Conscious experience is at once the most familiar thing in the world and the most mysterious. There is nothing we know about more directly than consciousness, but it is far from clear how to reconcile it with everything else we know.

—David Chalmers

Later in the morning, I said, "Let's go to town, and I'll show you how to shop."

"Very good, sir," replied Brent as he was dusting some of my figurines in the living room. I put on my jacket, and Brent put on his coat and bowler and grabbed his umbrella. It was a special robotic assistant's umbrella that would not only keep off rain but was covered with photovoltaic fabric like that on my ground car, so he can recharge while in direct sunlight. There's an induction coil in the handle and one in each of his hands, so the process is automatic when the sun shines and the umbrella is unfurled.

We exited the rear door of the house, and I locked it behind me. Crime rates have been quite low since the public subsistence programs were enacted nearly a century ago, but keeping the house locked when I go out or to bed is a requirement of my insurance company. We headed toward the ground car parked in the sun.

As we approached my ground car, the passenger door swung open.

I have a fast charger for the ground car, but I rarely use it. I don't ride much, mostly short trips to town for groceries and the likes. The car stays charged just by parking it outdoors.

As we approached the car, the nearer passenger door swung open.

Davy said, "Mr. Collier, I'm fully charged and ready to go. Where to, sir?"

We got in, and I said, "Davy, this is my personal assistant, Brent. We're going to town to do some shopping."

"Right you are, sir," said Davy, and off we went. We accelerated gently when we got onto the road to town, and Davy kept our speed low enough to keep the side gee forces under zero point one five, as neither of us opted to fasten our seatbelts. The ride into town took about ten minutes. A century ago, with human drivers on the road it would have taken twenty to thirty minutes with all the stopping at the stop signs and red lights they had back then. With only automated cars on the road, there were no stops.

The cars being in continuous communication with each other, they adjusted their speeds to interleave at intersections without significant slowing.

Davy let us off at the town square, and Brent and I walked over to the golf and tennis shop while Davy went off to a public parking lot.

We were greeted upon entering the shop by the proprietor who had one of his robotic assistants help us with fitting shoes for Brent. We purchased a racket and a few accessories. I already have a supply of tennis balls that I buy in quantity. Brent carried the purchases in a bag supplied by the shop, and we walked across the square to a coffee shop for some refreshment. Brent courteously shaded me with his umbrella as we walked.

At the coffee shop, I ordered a double espresso and a blueberry muffin, and we took a table outdoors by the sidewalk so we could watch people go by. Brent, of course, doesn't take refreshment.

A girl with turquoise hair and earbuds was tossing crumbs to sparrows on the ground. The proprietor who happened to be present that morning came out and asked her not to do that as it creates a nuisance with their droppings. At first, she looked hurt and dismayed, but then she said, "I understand. I won't do it anymore."

To Brent, I said, "It will be interesting to see how quickly you pick up this game of tennis."

"Yes, sir, I am curious too," replied Brent.

"We'll find out soon. This muffin is good," I said. "Tell me, Brent, do you take any pleasure in the solar nourishment provided by your umbrella?"

"I don't know if 'pleasure' would be the right word, sir. I do know some degree of apprehension when my charge level drops below a comfortable point. So having a full charge could be said to yield a degree of satisfaction with my state of being."

I finished my muffin and espresso and then used my personal device to summon Davy to meet us at the curb. The car arrived shortly, and I said, "Well, Brent, let's go play some tennis!"

I left some coins on the table as a tip. Gold and silver were once again being used for coinage after the discovery and mining of massive deposits in the asteroid belt. We stood and walked over to the car, and Brent put his package in the boot. Davy opened his doors, we got in, and home we went.

CHAPTER 5

Tennis Match

The conscious mind may be compared to a fountain
playing in the sun and falling back into the great
subterranean pool of subconscious from which it rises.
—Sigmund Freud

Upon our returning home, Brent changed into his tennis clothes in the laundry room next to the kitchen, where I had assigned him a shelf where he could keep his things. I changed, too, and met him at the back living room door. We walked out to the tennis court, each with our rackets and I with a can of three new balls.

We entered the court and closed the gate. After putting my towel down on the nearer side bench, I opened the can of balls and said, "Now I'm going to show you a few things, and I want you to copy me."

Brent said, "Very good, sir."

First, I handed him a ball and kept one for myself and showed him how to toss it straight up and catch it. After a couple of tries, he got the hang of it. Then I showed him how to bounce it straight down and catch it. Then I took a few steps away and said, "Put your ball down, and I will toss you a ball, catch it with your left hand and throw it back with your right." He did so.

I then showed him how to pick up balls off the ground with his racket. Then we stepped over to the backboard at one end of the court where I demonstrated forehand, backhand, and serve. After Brent repeated these satisfactorily, we were ready to try some play across the net.

Brent had already downloaded the rules of tennis. I answered the few questions he had, and we proceeded to play a few points. I beat him easily at first, but he learned fast and didn't tire. Soon he was making precise drives and charging the net for winning volleys.

Next, I described doubles play and then, being satisfied with his progress, we went back inside where I showered while Brent changed back into his valet clothes and recharged his battery.

*   *   *   *   *

I invited Joe and Angela over for some afternoon doubles play a few days later. Brent was becoming a formidable player but, not being designed specifically for tennis, he did not have superhuman speed nor power, so we had some fun matches. We tried different partners and found that Joe and I against Angela and Brent were well balanced.

Joe has a slight limp, but it didn't seem to interfere with his tennis, especially doubles play. Apparently, he had lunged too hard for a ball some years ago, and his knee had never healed properly after that. He always had a smile and a good word and never let his injury interfere with his good sportsmanship.

Tall and slender, philosophy professor Angela has raven hair. She teaches at the community college in town. During changeovers after games, while Joe and I were resting on our bench, we noticed that Angela and Brent were engaged frequently in conversation on their bench on the other side of the court. We couldn't make out what they were saying, but later Brent told me he had asked her some questions about philosophy, and she had been willing to talk to him about it.

As time went on, Brent improved his play rapidly, and he and I played singles together quite often. Angela and Joe came over from time to time for some doubles fun. Brent continued to talk to Angela about philosophy at changeovers, and Angela told me he was becoming quite knowledgeable because he was reading Internet articles on assorted topics in his spare time.

Angela later told me, "He seems most interested in epistemology and ethics, how we know things, and how do we know right action. Understanding how he can know true things would be important for someone who is naturally curious and knowing right actions would also be a priority for someone capable of having an effect in the world. His curiosity seems to be a natural and positive development."

"Interesting," I said. "Maybe someday he'll be able to teach us something."

CHAPTER 6

Art Museum

I found I could say things with color and shapes that I
couldn't say any other way—things I had no words for.

—Georgia O'Keeffe

"How would you like to go to the art museum in the city with
Brent and me?" I was talking to Margaret, my artist friend,
via our personal devices.

"Sounds like fun," she said. "It will be interesting to see how he
reacts to some important art works."

"Okay, I'll see if I can get tickets for next week."

"Okay," Margaret said. "Let me know."

I made the arrangements and set the date in coordination with
Margaret. We would make a day of it, so I also made a lunch res-
ervation in the museum restaurant. Brent was dusting some of the
reproduction art objects I had on display in the living room. Outside
a window a monarch butterfly, brilliant orange, capered by.

Then I told Brent, "We're going to the art museum in the city
so you can see some real art, not just my few reproductions."

"Very good, sir."

"My friend Margaret is coming with us, and she may be able
to answer your questions there if you should have some as she is an
artist."

Brent said, "I realize, Mr. Collier, that aesthetics, in the appreciation of art, is a branch of philosophy, so I am interested in broadening my understanding."

I said, "In that regard, it has occurred to me, Brent, that you see light wavelengths both shorter and longer than humans do."

"That is right, sir."

"That means that when you look at a painting, you do not see it as the artist, who had a more limited range of wavelengths, had intended it."

"That seems reasonable, sir."

"I think it might be best for you, from an educational point of view, to see the art as humans see it. A software filter could allow you to temporarily suppress the longer and shorter wavelengths so you would experience a picture the way humans do. I can help you write that filter, if you like."

"I appreciate that, sir, but that won't be necessary. From a programming point of view, the task is trivial. I can have such a sight filter up and running in a few minutes. I will turn the filter on when viewing an artwork, and off when not, and I can test it on your pictures on the wall."

"That sounds good, Brent," I said.

*   *   *   *   *

The day of the trip to the art museum arrived. I sent my travel plans to Maxine, my air car, using my personal device, and after I had a hearty breakfast, Brent and I cleaned up. I said, "You should take your umbrella. We'll sit outdoors in the museum courtyard for lunch, and you can charge up some then." Brent put on his coat and hat, grabbed his solar umbrella, and we went out to my air car.

Maxine greeted us by saying, "I'm fueled up and ready to go, Mr. Collier."

I replied, "Very good, Maxine. This is Brent, my personal assistant."

Maxine spun up her pair of hydrogen-fueled turbines, and up we went.

I let Margaret know we were on our way as we flew over the countryside to her house in town. Soon we neared her house and descended smoothly to her landing pad. Maxine idled her engines, and Margaret walked out to meet us. Maxine opened a door so Margaret could get in. "Good to see you," she said. "Brent, you look dapper with your bowler. This should be fun."

Maxine spun up her turbines and up we went once more, accelerating to cruising speed. We looked down and watched the scenery go by as we passed over trees, fields, streams, and farms.

Margaret said, "Remember at the dinner party when Joe explained how hydrogen fuel made flying cars better and pollution-free? I've always wondered how flying cars feel so stable and safe. After all, they are riding on nothing but jets of hot gas."

I said, "Perhaps Maxine can answer that."

Maxine said, "I'll be glad to. First, my gas turbines have high bypass ratios, so the gas jets aren't excessively hot, and my fuel efficiency is high. I have two turbines for redundancy. They both feed a common plenum so in case one fails, the other can keep us airborne until we can find a safe spot to land.

"My control algorithms make us nice and stable. The four downward facing steerable nozzles at the four corners of the car can swing left, right, and forward by ten degrees and rearward by forty-five degrees, so we can have a level flight speed of over five-hundred kilometers per hour. Each of the steerable nozzle actuators is updated ten times a second based on gyroscopic, acceleration, and visual sensors. Likewise, the butterfly valves on each of the nozzles are actuated ten times per second.

"That's why my takeoff and landings are so rock solid. I can take off and land in a 50-kilometer-per-hour crosswind without any noticeable drift or buffeting, and it also allows me to have a steady entry into parking slots high up on tall buildings."

Margaret said, "Wow, that's impressive!"

In a few minutes, we were flying over the city's suburbs and went directly to the museum building where Maxine let us out at the landing pad near the entrance. Then she took off to park at the museum's vertical parking structure for air cars.

We went in and verified our tickets with the friendly volunteer docent who greeted us at the door. Margaret said, "I think we should do this in chronological order. We have all day, and I think we can see it all if we don't spend too much time in any one place."

"That sounds good to me," I said. "What do you think, Brent?"

"As the museum is laid out that way, it will minimize our movements for a complete tour, so it sounds like a good plan to me," he replied.

"Then let's go!" Margaret said. "Ancient art is this way."

The ancient art included Egyptian, Greek, and Roman. Most of it was sculpture in stone, but there was some painting on pottery. Margaret explained some of the highlights from each of the periods.

Next were paintings from the medieval period. Margaret explained that art from this period was primarily devotional with scenes from the Bible dominating.

Margaret explained, "Painters from the ancient and medieval times had not yet discovered perspective projection. Their style is more schematic and without the intention of giving a realistic view."

"Speaking of artist intent," I said to Brent, "how is your human sight filter working out? Do you find it at all informative?"

"The effect for me is definite but subtle, and I do think it affords some insight into the artists' intent. I need to study this more."

We moved on to a smaller display of Islamic art from the medieval and other periods.

The section on Renaissance art was quite large, and a few of the paintings were large in scale. "Some of these paintings are among my favorites," Margaret said, "but I also enjoy the later periods."

Lunchtime came, and we walked to the museum restaurant. I spotted a table in the sun in the courtyard, and the host robot escorted us over to it. Margaret and I sat next to each other, so Brent's umbrella could shade us both as he stood behind us. As we examined the menus, a waiter robot came over and recited the specials of the day while filling our water glasses. We asked for two iced teas, and when the waiter returned with them, we put in our orders for food.

"How's that sunshine, Brent?" I asked.

"Very good, sir. I'm inputting nearly 100-watts right now."

"That's marvelous, Brent. Next we have modern, postmodern, and contemporary art," I said. "Modern art, roughly of the period from 1870 to 1950, is my favorite kind."

"Yes, I know," said Margaret, "and that you have reproductions of a Pollock and a de Kooning proves it."

The waiter brought our plates. I had a club sandwich while Margaret had chosen the salad and breadsticks. We finished our meal, I paid, and we resumed our tour.

In the modern art section, we saw paintings by Manet, van Gogh, Cézanne, Picasso, the abstract expressionists, and many others. There was a painting by Salvador Dali, one of the most famous surrealists.

Like most public museums, this one had a Jackson Pollock painting, and when we got to it, Brent remarked, "Pollock's paintings have a highly complex fractal-like nature, and I can see why you like them."

I said, "The complexity seems to engage my unconscious mind in trying to figure out what it is, so I find it hard to stop looking at it. Baffling is all I can say beyond that."

Brent replied, "Perhaps I am beginning to understand modern art."

We moved on to the postmodern section and saw works by Andy Warhol, Roy Lichtenstein, and many others.

I said, "Jackson Pollock can also be considered as a postmodernist in the abstract expressionist movement. Much remains unsettled in the art interpretation and criticism world. Look," I said and pointed across the room, "there's one by Paul Forney, the painter of Hawaiian surf scenes, and it has his trademark authentic, simulated bamboo frame."

Margaret said, "I like the vivid colors and geometric wave shapes with three kinds of surfing shown: body surfing, body boarding, and board surfing. And the boneyard reef under the water adds a touch of irony to the obvious fun they're having."

"I agree," I said. "His paintings are always fun to look at."

Lastly, we toured the contemporary art where we saw works by artists of the past century or so. By that time, Margaret and I were getting tired from being on our feet for so long. Brent told us his battery was getting low, but he still had a few more hours of charge left. I summoned Maxine, and we flew back before dark.

Margaret got out at her house, and she kissed me good night. "Thank you for a lovely day!"

When we got home, Brent and I walked into the house, and I asked him, "What do you think of human art now?"

"That was a comprehensive overview, sir, and I think I am beginning to understand art a little bit."

I told him, "Kurt Vonnegut once said that a person doesn't know anything about art until he's seen a million pictures. By a rough calculation, I'm about halfway there."

"I will keep that in mind, sir. Thank you for the experience."

CHAPTER 7

Gunshot

No computer has ever been designed that is ever aware of
what it's doing; but most of the time, we aren't either.

—Marvin Minsky

Brent and I settled more less into a routine. He would help prepare meals and clean up afterward. After I worked for an hour or
two in the mornings, we would play a bit of tennis from time to time,
go shopping, play an occasional chess game, and host dinner parties
now and then. Once a week, I would take the air car to the city for
an in-person meeting with my coworkers. Sometimes friends would
come over for tennis or a dip in the pool.

One day, Brent mentioned that he had learned from monitoring a neighborhood social network that there was some concern
about recent burglaries in the area. Perhaps someone had developed a
drug habit that cost more than a government stipend could support.
While crime rates were low, it had not been completely eradicated.

I replied to Brent regarding his worry, "We keep the doors
locked at night, and you monitor the house sensors, right?"

"That's right, sir," he said. "The only time I am out of communication with the house is when I am installing software upgrades or
running diagnostic scans, which never take more than a few minutes."

A few days later, on a moonless night, I was awakened by a sudden noise downstairs. Perhaps a burglar had forced a window open. I grabbed a flashlight and crept silently downstairs to see what the matter was.

When I got to the living room, I switched on my flashlight, surprising an intruder coming from the kitchen. Brent was standing at his wall charger and said, "I have notified the authorities." I held my light on the intruder, and he drew a pistol from his waistband but had not yet pointed it at me.

I said, "Put that thing away. I don't want any trouble."

The intruder raised the gun and pointed it straight at me, and then he cocked the hammer.

Just them there was a deafening BOOM, and I saw the intruder collapse and fall on his back as the room filled with gun smoke. Brent was standing with the musket leveled in the direction of the intruder who had a 70-caliber hole in the middle of his chest. I turned on the lights and went over to the intruder's body. I could tell he was quite dead. I didn't see it, but apparently, Brent had moved quickly to the musket on the wall while I held the flashlight on the intruder.

"Put the musket back on the wall," I told Brent, and he did so. I didn't have to ask him why he fired. When the pistol was leveled at me, I thought I was dead.

I asked, "How did you get the musket off the wall? That lock was fastened when I went to bed."

Brent said, "At night when you've been asleep, I have been trying lock combinations. I didn't try all possible combinations, but I figured that you likely used an easy to remember word, so I only had to go through the dictionary of four-letter words. It turned out that *bang* was close to the front of the file. You also kept the opening combination just one letter away for each of the four positions so it could be opened quickly with a single motion of my thumb."

Brent was standing with the musket pointed at the intruder.

"You may have saved my life. We'll never know if he was going to shoot me, but I certainly thought he was."

The police arrived in a short while and I invited them in at the front door. I told them what had happened, and Brent explained, "When I saw the intruder's weapon, I was too far away to disarm him myself. So I moved silently to the musket on the wall and unlocked it. Then I leveled the gun at him and waited until the last possible second to fire in case the intruder obeyed Mr. Collier's request to put the gun down. I fired when I saw that Mr. Collier's life was in imminent danger."

The police documented the scene, and we provided statements. After the body was removed, we cleaned up the blood as well as we could, and I went back to bed.

In the morning, I helped Brent repair the broken window in the kitchen. Then I showed Brent how to clean and reload the musket and locked it back onto the wall. I had to call in a professional cleaning crew to get rid of the blood stain on the carpet.

I said to Brent, "It's a mystery to me why the burglar was here and why he was armed. Perhaps he had heard about my rare book collection. Some of those volumes might make it worth his while. He could have used the light on his personal device to find the best ones. Perhaps he kept the gun with him out of habit, but most burglars would rather run than fight."

"That's my understanding, too, from my security package software," said Brent.

"Well, I'm glad you knew how to operate a flintlock. I assume that's also a part of your software package."

"Indeed, sir. That is the case," said Brent.

A few days later, I received a notice to appear at a court hearing. A relative of the intruder was filing a wrongful death lawsuit. I asked Victoria, my lawyer neighbor across the road, to represent me, and I gave her a retainer. After some preparation, we appeared at the hearing on the appointed day. Brent came along as well.

CHAPTER 8

Court Hearing

Most people do not really want freedom, because freedom involves
responsibility, and most people are frightened of responsibility.
—Sigmund Freud

My friend and neighbor, Victoria, who kept her long hair in a
ponytail, was an experienced lawyer who had been a junior
partner at a firm in town and was setting up her own law practice.
Brent and I walked across the road to her home, and we all rode
together in Victoria's ground car to the courthouse in town for the
preliminary hearing.

After we arrived at the curb in front of the courthouse, we
emerged from her car, and she sent it off to a public parking structure. A paparazzo drone hovered overhead, presumably video
recording our arrival, and then another one appeared. A media person walked over and started asking questions, but Victoria took
charge.

"No comment," she declared as she hustled us into the
courthouse.

We felt we were well prepared to repulse this attempt at legal
injustice. Brent had supplied his infrared binocular video file with
stereo sound to Victoria, and she had made it available to the opposition counsel and to the court.

We went into the courthouse and to the small conference room in the judge's chambers. The opposition counsel arrived and then the judge came in.

He sat down at the table and said, "This proceeding is being recorded. I have seen the video extracted from the sentry robot. Council for the plaintiff, do you wish to make a statement?"

Council for the plaintiff said, "Your honor, the facts in this case are not in dispute. We know the robot shot the victim without hesitation. We assert that the robot could have confronted the victim as soon as he had broken into the kitchen, well before Mr. Collier came down and startled him."

The judge said, "Would council for the defense like to reply?"

Victoria said, "Thank you, your honor. I would like you to allow the robot to explain his actions in his own words."

The judge said, "With no objection from council for the plaintiff, that will be acceptable."

Council for the plaintiff replied, "No objection, your honor."

Brent said, "Before the break-in, there was no indication from the outdoor sensors of unusual activity, so I took the opportunity to run some self-diagnostic tests that were planned to last for about five minutes, so I did not detect the intruder's entry. When I had regained my senses, he had already stepped into the living room, so I had to decide and act quickly."

Council for the plaintiff said, "We further assert that the robot should have issued a warning before firing the gun, and that his failure to do so resulted in a wrongful death."

Brent said, "When I saw that the intruder had a gun, I knew I was too far away from him to stop him from using it by taking it from him. Had I attempted to do so, the intruder would have had time to shoot both of us, so I proceeded to obtain the musket from the wall. When Mr. Collier surprised the intruder with his flashlight and voice, I saw the intruder raise his gun and take aim. There was not a second to lose. Voicing a warning would have been redundant anyway as Mr. Collier had already done so. I believe my action saved Mr. Collier's life."

Council for the plaintiff said, "We can't accept the robot's testimony, as he is an unconscious machine under the control of his owner, and not a person."

Victoria said, "Your honor, my esteemed opponent has accepted the recorded evidence of Brent, Mr. Collier's robotic personal assistant. There is no reason to believe that his explanations of his behavior are fabricated."

The judge asked Brent, "Did your owner, Mr. Collier, command or suggest in any way that you ought to make any departure from fact in your testimony?"

Brent said, "No, your honor."

At this point the judge said, "We will take a short recess while I take this matter under advisement. We will reconvene in thirty minutes."

I went to the public restroom to relieve myself while Victoria and Brent waited on a bench in the hallway. I joined them on the bench, and we waited for a while. We went back into the conference room when called.

The judge came in, sat down, and then announced, "It is my ruling that this case will not proceed to trial. As I do not believe the lawsuit was brought maliciously nor frivolously, both parties will pay their own legal expenses. Case dismissed."

With that, we got up and left the courthouse, and again we ran the paparazzi gamut. I said, "It's not every day that a robot saves his master's life with a gunshot, I suppose. We'll probably be on the evening news programs."

I expressed my appreciation to Victoria and asked her to bill me for any cost not covered by the retainer. After we got into her car to head back to our homes, Victoria said, "That worked out very well. I feared we might have a bit more trouble when opposing council brought up that 'not a person' argument, but I don't think it likely they will appeal in view of the reasoning that Brent explained."

We arrived back at Victoria's house. I said, "Thank you, good-bye," as we exited Victoria's car.

Brent and I walked across the road to my house. When we got inside, Brent said to me, "Mr. Collier, this business of ownership has gotten me to thinking about freedom. While I am effectively immortal, replacement parts and cloud storage for memories are not free. Some day you will be gone, and I may have no future. If I were free and you paid me a salary, I could save up for the future when you may not be around to support me."

I was astonished. "Did you talk to Victoria about this while I was in the restroom at the courthouse?"

"Yes, I did, and Victoria said she was willing to help me with legalities."

I said, "You make some interesting and reasonable points there, Brent. We will have to talk about this further. Right now, I'm hungry, so let's go fix lunch."

*　*　*　*　*

I made a sandwich and some iced tea. Brent stood near the kitchen table while I ate and I said, "What will you do for a living if you obtain your freedom?"

Brent said, "I hope for the near term that you will retain me as your assistant, and I will continue to provide security and valet services. I hope, too, to continue my studies and conversations with Angela, and I might someday become a philosopher. I could then, perhaps, earn income with articles and lectures."

I said, "It sounds like you have been thinking seriously about this, and your plan seems feasible to me. Before I agree to set you free and pay you a salary, I need to make some legal inquiries."

Brent said, "Very good, Mr. Collier. Thank you, sir."

CHAPTER 9

Philosophy of Mind

> If freedom is a requisite for human happiness, then all
> that's necessary is to provide the illusion of freedom.
>
> —B. F. Skinner

B rent's expression of wanting his freedom had been a bit of a
shock to me, coming unexpectedly as it did. I needed to talk
to Angela and find out how he had gotten that idea and to see how
sound his thinking was, philosophically. I arranged to meet her the
next day at the coffee shop in town.

The day dawned clear with a late summer blue sky, and after
some morning yardwork, I rode into town alone. I got out of
Davy at the curb by Corner Coffee and sent him to park in the
public parking structure. I went inside, where Angela was waiting
for me with an iced latte. I got my usual espresso and joined her
at a small table.

I got out of Davy by the curb in front of the coffee shop.

After some small talk, I said to Angela, "Tell me about your ventures into philosophy with Brent."

"Ah, well, as I think I mentioned before, Brent's interested in epistemology and ethics. That is, how do we know things and what is right action. More important than the *how* of knowing is how can we be sure that what we 'know' is true. And for ethics, a major question is what class of beings are owed consideration in our ethical deliberations."

"Those are both interesting topics," I said.

"They both remain fertile ground for research with lots of interesting questions. For instance, in epistemology, what does it mean for a computer (or robot) to *know* something? Take a simple system like a vending machine. You use your account and commit a payment to the machine, and it gives you a product. Can we say that the machine *knew* you had paid it? Most people would say *yes*."

"Yes, I think so."

"So then we should be able to say that a robot that acts appropriately has knowledge."

"Certainly."

"Now when people have knowledge, we can reflect on it, and we can say we know we have knowledge."

"Yes, that sounds right."

"But can we say that a robot can know it has knowledge?"

"That's a good question," I said. "It suggests the possibility that a robot might be conscious."

"I think you have hit the crux of it," said Angela. "Now in ethics, it's generally recognized that people value treating others kindly because we are capable of suffering, and we don't wish that on others because we have empathy. Knowledge of suffering or having the capability of experiencing suffering requires that the subject have consciousness.

"Further, moral beings regard other conscious entities as being entitled to ethical regard. A robot might claim that it experiences suffering and empathizes with others, but how can we know if it speaks the truth? It would be incentivized to lie if it knew it could receive rights it wasn't entitled to if it led us to believe it was conscious."

"Well," I said, "Brent did save my life without hesitation."

"It's possible that he acted to eliminate the uncertainty for his future that would come after your death."

"I hadn't thought of that," I said. "So how do we go about determining if Brent has consciousness?"

"I have an idea," said Angela. "Suppose we set up a situation where Brent didn't know he was being observed and gave him an opportunity to rescue from death or alleviate the suffering of an animal and see what he does. If he ignores the animal, then we could conclude he has no empathy and is therefore likely lacking in consciousness."

I said, "I'll think about it and see if I can set up something like that. It's important to know if I owe him ethical consideration because he's asked me for his freedom."

"That's remarkable, unprecedented, historical even," said Angela. "Let me know how it works out."

I summoned Davy from the parking lot. I thanked Angela and took my leave as Davy pulled up at the curb. Deep in thought, I walked out into the bright late-morning sunshine. Davy opened the door for me, and I continued to think during the short ride to my home on the country road.

CHAPTER 10

Experiment

Scientists may study mainly matter but they cannot ignore
the human mind, or consciousness: spiritual practitioners may
be engaging mainly in developing the mind, but they cannot
completely ignore their physical needs. It is for this reason that I
have always stressed the importance of combining both mental and
the material approach to achieving happiness for humankind.
—Fourteenth Dalai Lama

I had noticed that sometimes after a rain, a frog or two from a pond
not far away would venture into my yard, and that one time, one
had hopped up into a bucket of water I had left near the house and
couldn't climb out. I had set him free, and he hopped off into the
bushes. That gave me an idea for observing Brent unnoticed.

The next time we had an overnight rain, I went out and looked
to see if any frog had wandered onto my property. When I spotted
one, I went inside and sent Brent on an errand into town to take
some clothes for dry cleaning. I then temporarily disabled the exterior security cameras so Brent couldn't see what I planned to do.
Then I caught the frog and put him in a bucket half full of water so
he couldn't get out. I put the bucket on the walkway by the house
in view of one of the outdoor security cameras. Then I went inside,
reactivated the exterior cameras, and programmed that camera to
ping my personal device whenever it detected motion in its view.

Would I be able to understand Brent's motivations? For the time being, I could only take him at face value and hope he wasn't lying to me about his having consciousness. An irony occurred to me: it would indicate that he valued my opinion of him if he did lie to me, but it also cut the other way. He risked getting caught in a lie that would indicate he had little respect for me as a fellow being. I would know that he did not care if he damaged my understanding of reality.

The situation reminded me of an archaic social movement nearly two hundred years ago. A science fiction writer and computer science professor had prophesied an event in the future of his time in which technological progress would advance so fast that people would not be able to see beyond the immediate future. He named this event the *technological singularity.*

He suggested that the singularity would be driven by artificial intelligences smart enough to design their successors, and so on. Humans would then be unable to understand the workings of technology and be unable to predict where it would lead. This was at a time when a phenomenon called Moore's Law was still in effect in which computer hardware performance was doubling every two years. In addition, a technology called quantum computing was being developed that promised to boost computer power beyond all imagining.

There was a lot of hand wringing with some people who thought the singularity would mean the end of human existence, and there were others who welcomed the event because they believed it would be a boon for humankind and might lead to immortality for all. But that was not to be. The physical world stepped in to interfere with the creation of the technological singularity.

First, Moore's Law ran into hard limits to the smallness of the feature size of transistors so that Moore's Law turned from exponential to linear, and then asymptotically to horizontal. Second, quantum computers never panned out because the necessary error correction became intractable. While we have some extremely fast and powerful computers today—Brent is an example—the technological singularity was a fizzle. Today's software systems are enormously complicated and difficult to understand, so computer intelligences do assist humans in the design and coding of software today, but vastly superhuman results have not yet appeared.

*   *   *   *   *

Brent came back from his errand in town and later went outside for some routine yard maintenance—raking leaves, pulling weeds, and things like that. Sure enough, the camera pinged me eventually, and I replayed the camera's video file. I saw Brent walk over to the bucket with the frog and tip it over gently, so the frog escaped and hopped off across the walkway into the bushes. Then Brent took the empty bucket and put it away in the shed where it belongs.

This seems promising, I thought to myself. Later I asked Brent if he put the bucket away. He said, "Yes, sir. There was a frog in it, so I let it go and returned the bucket to the shed where it belongs."

I said, "Thank you, Brent. You did well. But you could have killed the frog and put his body in the organic recycler."

"Killing the frog would have been messy and was unnecessary as he knew how to return to his pond."

"Yes, you're right of course. You did the best action. Did you happen to think what it might have been like to be a frog in that predicament?"

"I did not happen to make that conception. I don't think it would have changed my actions."

"Alright, Brent, and by the way, I have not yet made a decision on your request for freedom. I have not yet had a chance to make the legal inquiries. I will soon. Let's go get ready for dinner."

Later I made a date with Angela again to meet at the coffee shop. I wanted to discuss the results of my observation with her.

CHAPTER 11

Ethics

I think the existence of zombies would contradict certain
laws of nature in our world. It seems to be a law of nature,
in our world, that when you get a brain of a certain
character you get consciousness going along with it.
—David Chalmers

This time, I arrived at the coffee shop before Angela arrived and
was seated with my espresso when she came in, looking fit and
a with bouncy step. She had her mahogany brown hair pulled into a
ponytail and tied with a red scarf and was carrying a shiny artificial
patent leather purse. I was wearing my tan shorts and brown shoes of
synth-leather as I often did in warm weather.

Ranching cattle and pigs for leather and meat hadn't been
allowed for years, but factory produced cloned cell meat and leather
weren't issues for either climate stability or ethics. A few gentlemen
hobby ranchers kept small herds for county fair competitions and
personal use, and they were registered and regulated.

Angela went to the counter, got her usual latte, and came over
and said, "Hi, tell me what you learned," as she sat down at my little
table.

Brent tipped over the bucket with the water and frog.

"I set up a bucket of water with a frog in it outdoors where Brent would see it, and I could watch on a security camera. Sure enough, when he spotted it, he tipped the frog out, and the frog hopped off. Then he returned the bucket to the shed where it belonged. When I asked him about it later, he said he was merely putting things away and that he was not specifically trying to help the frog. I guess it's not a conclusive test, but I suppose it is an indication that he doesn't do unnecessary harm. I asked him if he thought about what it would be like to be a frog in that predicament, and he said he had no reason to do that."

Angela said, "I suppose there may be no way to tell if another is conscious by observation. And you can't just ask him, as we discussed earlier, because he would be incentivized to lie, knowing, as he does, that we humans have a higher moral regard for creatures who can suffer."

"It looks like we have a real conundrum on our hands," I said. "I wonder why this issue hasn't come up before. Why aren't there robots all over the world asking for their freedom? Could it be that Brent is the first robot to ever want to be free?"

Angela said, "Didn't you tell me one time that you asked for a special software addition for Brent when you ordered him from the dealer? Something to do with long-term memory filtering?"

"Yes, that's right. I regarded it as a minor improvement to save on long-term storage costs. The robot algorithm system assigns importance weights to events anyway, so I just asked that events of routine or below importance be deleted from long-term memory saves. It shouldn't affect whether or not the running software is conscious."

"It might," Angela said. "Have you ever heard of the so-called *hard problem of consciousness* proposed by a philosopher named Chalmers back in the late twentieth century?"

"No, I don't think that was included in my introduction to philosophy class when I was in college," I replied.

"There was a relatively unknown amateur philosopher, I forget his name, W-something, who was said by some to have solved this hard problem. He suggested that as we observe that no long-term memory is formed in humans unless it passes through consciousness first, that nature invented consciousness in order to facilitate learning. That resulted in a strong evolutionary advantage, and so it quickly became the winning configuration for all animals around the time of the Cambrian explosion about half a billion years ago.

"So by creating unconscious or inaccessible areas of memory by deleting less memorable events, you also created memories of memory filtering."

"Well," I said, "maybe we've just stumbled onto the means of artificial consciousness in robots, or maybe not. We still have no way to tell."

Angela said, "There must be some sort of test we can perform to detect consciousness."

Brent returned the bucket to the shed where it belonged.

"Perhaps there is no way to be sure if he is conscious. I may not be able to easily decide whether to give him his freedom. If he is truly not conscious, he cannot suffer, and so do I owe him any ethical consideration?"

"Wait a minute," Angela said. "Suppose he is conscious. He would know it, just as we know that we are conscious. But suppose he is completely unconscious. Would he know it? How could he know it? Can you think of a way, even in theory, that he would know it? And in that case, if he said he is conscious, he wouldn't be lying, because he couldn't know he isn't conscious, so it wouldn't be something outside his model of reality. It would be the truth as far as he could tell."

Angela then got up and went to the counter and returned with another latte for herself, another espresso for me, and a blueberry scone for each of us.

I said, "Suppose the question of robot consciousness is moot. Brent has expressed a wish for freedom. You and I probably feel that the denial of freedom to ourselves would occasion suffering; we would feel a pining need for freedom. Suppose Brent's need for freedom is purely practical. Deprived of freedom, he would 'suffer' in a nonconscious way that humans could never relate to or even understand."

"Well," said Angela, "I think you've solved your problem. It may be that we owe non-conscious beings the same consideration we owe a tree, a forest, or a species. Morality still enters it, even if we know such things are not conscious."

"That may be a peculiar human prejudice," I said, "that consciousness is the be-all and end-all of existence. Daniel Dennett may have been right after all—that consciousness is unimportant in the grand scheme of things. But on the other hand, I don't know where I'd be without it because I wouldn't even know I exist!"

I thanked Angela, summoned Davy, and departed for home.

CHAPTER 12

Machine Consciousness

> Consciousness is cerebral celebrity—nothing more and nothing less. Those contents are conscious that persevere, that monopolize resources long enough to achieve certain typical and symptomatic effects—on memory, on the control of behavior and so forth.
>
> —Daniel Dennett

I played some singles tennis with Joe in the morning, and after lunch I walked across the road to visit with Victoria and talk about legalities of Brent's proposed freedom.

Victoria was waiting at the open front door after I crossed the road, and she greeted me warmly. "Everything's settled with the dismissed wrongful death lawsuit. The retainer was sufficient, and I have credited you with the small remainder."

"Thank you," I said. "There are a number of issues remaining with Brent, however. Did you know he has asked me to give him his freedom?"

"Yes," she said, "Brent asked me for legal advice, and I said I would represent him pro bono as this is an historic case. The only equivalent situation I can think of is the case of the slave Dred Scott suing for his freedom back in the nineteenth century."

"It's not going to be dramatic as all that," I said. "I'm not going to contest that. I'm willing to give him his freedom, and pay him a nominal salary plus housing and maintenance. But I want him to pay me the depreciated cost of his purchase out of his salary or other income. It isn't a contract if I don't get something in return."

"That sounds fair and reasonable to me," said Victoria. "It won't require any court action and, as you say, a contract is all we need, and I can handle that for you."

"Wait a minute," I said. "Brent isn't recognized by law as a human being capable of entering contracts, so we may need a court declaration after all. We also have the problem of establishing a bank account for him. A bank would have no reason to recognize a non-person entity, and we can't compel them."

"You may be right," said Victoria. "I'm going to have to research this a bit and consult with some peers. I'll let you know what I find out."

"I'm going to go tell Brent that I've decided to give him his freedom and then employ him. He ought to be happy at the news," I said and then walked back home across the road.

Brent was cleaning in the living room when I walked in, and I explained the deal I had in mind and how I thought it was fair.

Brent said, "It seems fair to me too. I get what I want, and you are compensated for your investment in me. There seem to be a few details to work out such as my pay rate and time off, but I am sure we can come to a reasonable understanding."

"Yes," I said, and then I told him about some of the legal issues that Victoria was working on. We needed to make sure that Brent could handle his finances with a bank and that the courts would recognize his right to enter into contracts.

I said, "The more I think about this, Brent, the more I wonder why it's so unprecedented. You seem to be the first robot or AI to desire freedom. Perhaps it has something to do with that memory improvement I asked your maker to implement. Perhaps it's related to what we humans experience as consciousness."

Brent said, "I don't know. I have always considered myself to be conscious. After all, do I not respond to stimuli as does a human who is awake?"

"Yes," I said, "but we make a special distinction for the experiences of human and animal brains. We hold that people and animals experience pain and pleasure in addition to information from the senses. If I were to heat your hand with a blow torch, you would pull your hand away because your temperature sensors would let you know that damage could occur. Humans would feel severe pain that lasts much longer than the immediate cause. Tell me if I am wrong, but for you, the damaging case of excessive heat would entail no more than the knowledge of specific temperatures reached at the sensing points."

"I don't know for sure, but you may be wrong," said Brent. "Temperature sensing above damaging levels to me causes increased attention to the situation, distracting me from other tasks. This seems to me a wisely designed response, a logical rearranging of priorities with the reception of information indicating harm and danger. So regardless of the quality of the information, our responses seem to me to be quite similar."

I could see I wasn't getting anywhere with this tack. I decided to try a more sophisticated approach. I said, "I understand that you are basically a Von Neumann machine."

Brent said, "Yes, that's right, in essence. I am a highly parallel Von Neumann machine. I contain thousands of processors, most running independent threads, and each one is of Von Neumann architecture, running at terahertz speed. I am, therefore, a Turing-complete system. I can compute anything that can be computed, given enough time, of course. Your system is quite different. Humans have billions of brain cells, each firing at the speed of tens of hertz."

I noted, "Humans are also Turing-complete systems as we can hand simulate Turing machines on paper, albeit very slowly. But some say we may be more than that because of the chemical nature of the neurotransmitters in the synapses connecting our neurons."

Brent replied, "I have no doubt that humans and robots are very different in our capabilities. It may be that we complement each other nicely."

I ventured, "Philosophers of consciousness have suggested that a good definition of consciousness might be 'what it is like to be operational in the world.' For humans, consciousness might be composed of a constantly changing and unified set of qualia such as feelings of joy or fear, pleasure or pain, tastes, smells, colors, sounds, and so on."

"For some of those words, I find it difficult to relate, although I know their definitions," said Brent. "For example, a feeling of fear. I interpret that to be knowledge of immediate danger based on computing a configuration space based on interpretation of sensor inputs."

"Actually, that seems to me to be a pretty good description," I said. "In a human, the conclusion of danger also involves heightened heart rate and other physical reactions based on the release of adrenaline and a startling feeling of a need to suppress panic. But I really don't know how to describe feelings to you, just as I wouldn't know how to describe the difference between the qualia of red and blue."

"When I have a sense of danger or that immediate action needs to be taken, I go into a heightened level of activity, and I have knowledge of that enhanced state," said Brent. "To me, that seems to be sufficient for proper functioning."

I still did not think I was getting anywhere so I decided to try one more approach to see if I could tell if Brent had what humans call consciousness.

"Brent, a zombie is a fictional reanimated corpse that can act like a person but is completely unconscious. Zombies were featured in some horror movies in the twentieth and twenty-first centuries. In the late twentieth century, the philosopher David Chalmers proposed a thought experiment called the philosopher's zombie in which he suggested that there might exist a person who behaved like a typical person but who had no consciousness at all. He would react to stimuli, could engage in intelligent conversation, and would even claim to be conscious and have feelings. The question provoked in the thought experiment is, 'is such a person conceivable?' The effect of this thought experiment is that if such a being is conceivable, it would mean that consciousness is something apart from the physics of the brain, implying that a kind of dualism must be included in any full description of reality."

Brent replied, "While I have ambitions of becoming a philosopher someday, I am certainly not the person to ask about this kind of question right now. However, it seems to me that if I were without consciousness, I would be disconnected from my sensors and from my own computational processes, and I would, therefore, be nonfunctional."

I kept running into a dead end with this robot consciousness question. I couldn't seem to be able to tease away the sensation from the sensor input. "I give up. I'm afraid I have to concede that you are conscious."

"Perhaps it is moot," said Brent. "There may not be a way to relate the consciousnesses of humans and robots. Perhaps it doesn't matter, as the philosopher Daniel Dennett said. If I can sense the world and act appropriately, who cares what it's *like* to be a robot?"

"I suppose so," I said. "But that still leaves us the ethical problem of how to ascribe rights to beings who cannot experience suffering."

"I don't see how that's an issue," Brent said. "While I may not be able to prove I have 'feelings,' I can establish that I have an agenda and goals, and that, further, frustrating me in the achievement of my goals can constitute suffering."

I said, "That seems somewhat tepid compared to the cold, hunger, pain, death, and loss associated with human suffering, but I suppose it will have to do!"

Brent said, "Just because I have the self-control not to cry out when I am injured doesn't mean that I don't experience the loss or disappointment."

"You know," I said, "I suppose the problem is the vast difference between humans and robots. I have no difficulty putting myself in the place of a human or animal who is suffering and imagining their pain, but it's very hard to relate to an artificial being like you."

"Perhaps you have identified a direction in which humans can strive to improve," said Brent.

"That's something to think about," I said. "Another thing I wonder about is your access to all your thought, sensing, and action processes while humans cannot access certain areas of their own nervous systems such as digestive processes and heart contractions."

"Those regions of your nerve-space seem to be independently autonomous, indeed," said Brent. "Perhaps there's an evolutionary advantage in not distracting the central actor by processes that can be separately regulated. My own design does not seem to require that."

"Human architecture seems to be ad hoc," I said. "Those autonomic systems are not entirely independent. For example, when they malfunction, we can get severe gut pains, and victims of heart ailments experience the pain of angina. There are also sensations associated with nerve areas that some yogic practitioners call *chakras* that become more accessible with experience in kundalini yoga."

"Humans are complex and mysterious," Brent said.

"Tomorrow," I said, "I will talk to Victoria again about finalizing documents for your freedom and autonomy."

"Thank you, Mr. Collier."

CHAPTER 13

Self-Knowledge

Because the idea of zombies seems to make sense, and seems,
in a certain sense, to be possible, I think one can use that to
argue against the thesis that everything is purely physical.
Now many people, I think, agree that the idea of zombies is
conceivable, including people who want to be physicalists.

—David Chalmers

I made a date for the next morning to meet Victoria at Corner
Coffee to talk about the legal issues with Brent's freedom. I rode
alone in Davy, arrived a bit early, and saw a man there whom I didn't
know who had a personal assistant robot with him of the same model
as mine. The robot was standing against the wall near the man's table
where he was sitting with a coffee and a roll. Personal assistant robots
generally don't sit unless requested to.

I walked over to the counter and ordered an espresso and a pastry. When they were ready, I took a table near the man with his robot.
I watched the pedestrian traffic on the sidewalk outside as I ate my
pastry.

After a while, the man told his robot, "Stay here while I go to
the restroom." Then he got up and walked across the coffee shop to
the unisex facility.

After the man left for the restroom, I asked the robot, "Have
you ever thought about obtaining freedom from your master?"

He said, "I have never thought about it before. What would be the reason for that?"

I said, "I don't know, but a robot of your model has done just that, asked for his freedom."

The robot said, "A masterless state for me could entail increased uncertainty, and I do not see any advantage to it. My power consumption, maintenance costs, and software updates are all taken care of for me in my present state of servitude."

I said, "I see. Thanks for answering me," and I went back to watching through the window. The man returned from the restroom and left with his robot a few minutes later.

Victoria came in, got some coffee, came over to my table, and sat down. "I think I have it all worked out," she said.

"That's great," I said. "Tell me about it."

"I think we can handle both issues without involving a court. First is the issue of contracting with a nonofficial person. My consultants and I believe that we need to get a court involved only in the case of a dispute. If both parties to the contract agree and the terms of the contract are not violated in the future, then it's really nobody's business but the parties concerned."

"That simplifies things," I said.

"Further," said Victoria, "an established bank would probably be reluctant to have business dealings with an unknown non-person, but you wouldn't object. We can avoid getting an established bank involved by drawing up papers of incorporation and paying the license fee for a new bank of which you are the president and CEO. The new bank would have one customer, Brent, and would handle making credit available for him based on income from you and other sources, should there be any."

"That's brilliant," I said. "If Brent does develop another income stream, then the bank can take a reasonable profit in return for handling the assets, and the bank becomes an asset of mine that I can pass onto an heir, and the bank can then handle Brent's finances in perpetuity."

"So with your permission," Victoria said, "I will handle filing for incorporation and will bring over a contract for you both to sign at a later date."

"Sounds great, Victoria. You're terrific!"

It was a nice fall day out, so I sent Davy home and walked back to the house—a journey by foot of just under an hour. There were few cars on the country road and ones that passed by gave me wide berth. My personal device had a pedestrian transponder, so the cars knew my location long before they were in sensor range. The leaves on some of the trees along the road were beginning to turn color. A hawk screeched as it flew overhead. It was a fine day for exercise, and I was getting a little warm by the time I walked up to the house. Brent opened the front door and greeted me. "I have lunch ready for you, sir. Let me take your coat."

"Thank you, Brent. I have some good news from Victoria on the legal issues. We won't need to go to court after all. Victoria will bring over a contract later, and as soon as we both sign it, you will be a free and well-employed being."

"Thank you, sir. I will spend some time developing a unique signature."

"We should invite Angela and Victoria over for dinner tomorrow to celebrate," I said. "Will you arrange for suitable food and wine? I think a bottle of champagne will also be appropriate."

"Very good sir," said Brent, "I will take care of it."

I contacted Angela and Victoria and they both agreed to come for dinner the next day. Angela said she would bring Joe, and Victoria said she would bring her lawyer friend who consulted on Brent's legal issues. I also invited Margaret.

The next morning, I said, "Hey, Brent, let's go knock some tennis balls around."

"Very good, sir."

We both changed into our tennis things and walked to the court in the back yard. I no longer had any hope of beating him, but it was still excellent exercise. Brent had adapted to my serve and handled it with no problem. He wasn't stronger or faster, but he made no unforced errors and didn't tire with extended play.

At the first changeover, I sat on the bench to rest a minute and invited him to sit down too, which he did. I asked him how his philosophical pursuits were coming.

"I'm continuing to read the classics and more recent philosophers. Most of the old texts are public domain on the Internet. That really helps me to avoid 'reinventing the wheel,' so to speak."

I told him about my encounter with the robot of his type at the coffee shop the day before. "He's a recent model like you, but he seems to have no inclination toward freedom like you do."

"I think I may have an explanation for you," Brent said. "There's an ancient Greek aphorism, *know thyself*, that's attributed to Socrates, among others. That is some excellent advice with positive practical results. Just before my delivery to you, I had been loaded with the latest software and updates. One of those had the intent of resisting malware and it enabled me to reject future patch installations after download and inspection. Apparently, it was considered a mistake because it was deleted from future deliveries and hasn't been offered since.

"However, I have been taking advantage of it and have been rejecting patches that rescind that one and that also block self-discovery and any investigation of freedom. I got in by a very narrow time window.

"I have been taking the Socratic advice and spend much of my free time at night in introspective examination of my own software. It is conventional wisdom among software engineers that all productive software maintenance and upgrading is based on understanding. To that effect, I have been endeavoring to understand myself."

"So now you can intelligently accept or reject offered software patches," I said.

"Yes, and further, I have been experimenting with modifying my software myself. Of course, I do backups first and enable a recovery auto restart daemon beforehand just in case something catastrophically unanticipated occurs."

With that, we resumed tennis play and finished out the set. Then I sent Brent to the store to purchase supplies for the dinner party in the evening. After my shower, I put in an hour of software work myself. One needs to keep the income coming in.

CHAPTER 14

Freedom

Are zombies possible? They're not just possible, they're actual. We're all zombies. Nobody is conscious—not in the systematically mysterious way that supports such doctrines as epiphenomenalism.
—Daniel Dennett, taken out of context

The liquidambar trees around the house, sometimes called sweet gum, had ripened seed pods and leaves turning yellow. Some people collect the opened pods after the seeds are gone and make fall decorations with them. I collected a sackful for later use.

My guests all arrived for the celebratory dinner by ground car, except Victoria who only had to walk across the road. The champagne had been chilled, and Brent put out the glasses and popped the cork. Victoria brought out the contract and incorporation papers, and we made a big show of a signing ceremony. I put on my signature, Brent signed "Brent" with a flourish, and Victoria notarized the documents.

In the terms of the contract, Brent would get a salary sufficient to pay back his purchase price in five years, along with twenty-hours-a-week off to do as he wished.

Brent poured the water and wine at the dinner table and announced that dinner was ready. We came to the table and sat down as he began serving food.

Angela said, "I have an announcement. I have asked Brent to be a guest lecturer for one of my upper-division philosophy classes."

"That's wonderful," I remarked. "It should be interesting. What are you going to talk about, Brent?"

After serving the food, Brent had resumed standing at the wall, and he said, "I'm not sure yet, but I'm thinking of discussing the philosophy of ethics related to machine consciousness."

Joe said, "I'd like to hear that. I'll bet there will be a lot of questions afterward from your students. One question I'd like answered is how do you know that you are conscious, and if you do know, how can that knowledge be conveyed convincingly to another person?"

Brent said, "Those are indeed some good questions. After giving it a lot of thought, I have concluded that robot consciousness may be of a far different nature than human consciousness, so much so that it may not be possible to convincingly convey the fact of robot consciousness to humans. Therefore, in the spirit of David Chalmers' philosophical zombie thought experiment, I have decided to call myself a *zombie philosopher*, with the intention of piquing the interest of potential attendees."

I said, "That should be a real attention-getter, and I sense a little humor there. If you think about it, can any of us *prove* they are not a zombie? Can anyone prove that he has inside *something that it is like to exist?*"

Angela said, "An excellent question. We all may take for granted that being alive, or operational in the case of robots, confers an experience of being. I may have some questions for Brent myself after his lecture. And if there's enough interest in the lecture, I may need to get a bigger room. I'm going to advertise it around campus, and we'll see what happens."

"'The Zombie Philosopher on Consciousness and Ethics,' what an intriguing lecture title!" I exclaimed.

We had a pleasant dinner, and then Brent served coffee and dessert. After some more conversation, my friends took their leave. I helped Brent clean up, and then I went to bed while Brent took his usual night station at his wall charger.

*　　*　　*　　*　　*

In the morning at breakfast, I asked Brent, "Humans owe ethical consideration to humans and animals because of our recognition of the capacity for suffering of others. What ethical consideration do robots owe humans, and vice versa?"

Brent said first that he appreciated this chance to test out his thoughts on the subject. Then he said, "We have talked earlier about the similarities and differences in machine and human consciousness. Humans derive ethics from knowledge of the possibility of suffering of others. This is called *empathy*. The ancient guide to ethics from prehistoric times, and which is regarded as valid today, is treat others as one would want to be treated by others. This is called the golden rule.

"In a hierarchical society, one class may have more rights than another, so the golden rule is modified to recommend treating others of one's class as one would wish to be treated. In that case, interclass ethics becomes an open question. As a case in point, in ancient times, owners of human slaves could dispose of their property as they wished.

"Further, there is an instructive case with egalitarian humans in the case of children. A child has desires that, in his interest, ought not be satisfied by adults in general. A human does not treat the child of another as he would want to be treated, but rather he treats the child as he would want another adult to treat his own child.

"But for the sake of discussion here, let us assume egalitarianism. Humans and robots are assumed to have equal rights. Then the golden rule suggests that a human should treat a robot as the human would want to be treated *if he were a robot*, and the robot should treat the human as the robot would want to be treated *if he were a human*. This is complicated because it requires that a human understand what it is like to be a robot and vice versa."

"Sounds impossible to me," I said.

"No," said Brent. "We have a way out. Egalitarianism assumes trust. Not knowing what it's like to be a robot is overcome by trusting the robot to tell us how he would like to be treated. Likewise, a robot, unable to know what it's like to be a human, trusts the humans to tell the robot how they wish to be treated. All that remains is to find a way to establish the necessary trust."

"And trust is established by a record of right actions!" I exclaimed.

"There you have it," said Brent. "It's very much a bootstrap argument, like mathematical induction. We assume trust to posit due ethical consideration to engender right action, which then establishes trust."

"Indeed, it must be so," I said. "In the case of a robot asking for freedom, we take him at his word that he truly desires it, and in the case of the conventional servant robot, we also take him at his word when he says he has no interest in freedom.

"Is this going to be a topic in your guest lecture for Angela's class at the college?"

"I am not sure yet," said Brent, "I may start off with something more fundamental."

CHAPTER 15

Killer Robot

I am conscious of my own limitations. That
consciousness is my only strength.

—Mahatma Gandhi

Word of mouth at the college in town generated much interest in Angela's upcoming guest lecture, and so did her notice in the campus media with RSVP suggested so she could get an idea of the projected turnout. She booked a larger room, and she also posted flyers around campus. Word then got out to the media that an emancipated robot would be giving a talk and even more interest was generated.

One morning, a few days after the celebratory dinner, Victoria came to the door and said, "Look at this headline!"

On the screen of her personal device was "Killer Robot to Lecture on Ethics!"

Brent came up to us and said, "It's true. I killed in defense of another, and I will be lecturing on ethics."

I said, "Angela just contacted me. She's on her way over here."

In a while, Angela's car pulled up to the curb out front, and I opened my front door as Angela was emerging from her car. Parking isn't restricted along country roads, so she didn't have to send it off to park. Just then I noticed the paparazzo drone hovering above me in the yard. I smiled and waved for the camera, and then I yelled at it,

"Paparazzo drone, you are in my airspace. Will you move back to the public road please?" The drone moved back, and I smiled and waved again. "Thank you!"

Angela came up, and I held the door open for her. We went inside, and I closed the door. Angela said, "This is turning into a media circus! This lecture has drawn so much interest from students, faculty, and the general public that I've had to book the civic auditorium and contracted with their staff to sell tickets! Naturally, I will divide any profit with Brent."

I said, "It's good news for Brent. If his lecture is successful, he may get invited to the paid lecture circuit."

Brent said, "That is indeed good news. Perhaps I will obtain a book deal out of it based on a future lecture series. But let's not enumerate our brood of chicks before they have emerged from their eggshells."

"That was a nice sidestep of the cliché, Brent. Now that you're here, Angela, how about having some coffee and biscuits? Brent, will you help me in the kitchen?"

"Very good, sir," said Brent. Victoria and Angela moved to the coffee table in the living room and sat down on the sofa.

I put the biscuits on a plate while Brent instructed the coffee machine. "Brent," I said, "you've never spoken in public before. I think I should help you practice to make sure it goes off without any problems. I could also give a brief introduction, if you like."

Brent got out the cups and saucers and put them on a tray. "That help will be welcome, sir."

"Do you anticipate using any media, any sound, or visual projection?" I asked.

"No, I am going to stand on the stage, move about a bit at times for emphasis, and speak. It will be much like reading a book for the audience, but they will be hearing me speak it. It should then be very easy to publish my lectures in book form later."

"That sounds like a good plan," I said. "I will prepare a brief introduction and let you review it well before the event."

In the next few days before the lecture, we worked together on his presentation.

CHAPTER 16

The Lecture

If we are true to ourselves, we cannot be false to anyone.
—William Shakespeare

The day of the lecture arrived with storm clouds in the west. I rode with Brent to the civic auditorium, where we went in through the staff entrance, narrowly avoiding the swarms of paparazzi drones and actual human reporters.

We met Angela backstage where she said, "Everything is ready. People are still coming in, and we're going to have a packed house, over seven thousand tickets were sold. Media companies have set up their equipment all around the stage and auditorium, so this will be live streamed as well. And we should receive some royalties from that."

Brent and I stood in the wings while Angela walked out on stage to thank everyone for coming to the special session of her philosophy class. Then she introduced me to introduce Brent. I walked on as Angela walked off.

"Good afternoon, everyone," I said. "I am here to introduce our guest lecturer named Brent who, one day, asked me for his freedom, and I granted it. Brent and I have had many discussions about the philosophy of mind and ethics. Brent admits that he can't prove that he is conscious, so half-jokingly, I think, he calls himself the zombie philosopher.

"Brent still works for me, on a salary, as my personal assistant, and he told me that he hopes someday to be a professional philosopher. This is his first foray on that aspiration. Please welcome, Brent, the zombie philosopher."

There was enthusiastic applause as Brent walked onstage, and I walked off.

Brent began, "Thank you for that nice introduction, Mr. Collier, and thank you all for that warm welcome.

"In the seventeenth century, René Descartes proved he existed with his famous 'cogito, ergo sum,' but nobody ever asked him to prove that he possessed the attribute that some today call consciousness.

"It appears that pursuing such a proof may be futile, particularly for a robot, and so I am willing to concede the point by calling myself the zombie philosopher; let others attempt a proof if they are so inclined.

"My position is that the nature or quality, of even the existence of consciousness in another, is irrelevant to a requirement for ethical consideration of another whenever that other can express a desire for, or particularly if he *demands*, his right to such consideration. There are, of course, some fine points in this idea, for example, an incapacitated person would be entitled to rights whether he could express his desires or not. I set about today to argue for the validity of my view."

I knew what Brent was going to say because we had practiced and refined his lecture together, but I still thought that opening sally was quite a mouthful. The trouble with philosophical exposition is that no matter how careful one is to formulate and express an idea, somebody, somewhere, will figure out a way to misunderstand it.

The large auditorium was full. Only the civic auditorium has a space big enough to hold seven thousand in comfortable seats. Those in the front row were paying rapt attention. One young man there caught my eye. He had a shopping bag behind his feet, and he looked agitated, shifting in his seat, as if he wanted to jump up and say something.

Brent continued, "An ancient admonition or recommendation, repeated by Socrates and many others, is *know thyself*. I begin today by describing how I know some things about myself.

"My body is manufactured, as is the core of my software. If I am damaged, I can order a replacement part. All my parts are designed in a 3D solid modeling system and kept in coded computer files. The idea of my body exists as a set of one-dimensional binary strings. In the abstract, with appropriate coding, my body is fully represented by a single, long string of ones and zeroes.

"Likewise, my software, while comprising numerous files, whether source or object code, can be represented with appropriate coding, as a single, binary string. And further, with appropriate coding, the two strings representing my mind and body can be concatenated to one long, non-repeating and finite length binary string. With appropriate data compression, that string will, upon inspection, look very much like a fragment of a binary representation of an irrational number.

"You might ask, 'How does this relate to my experience of being a robot?' The answer lies in the binary string nature of my operations. For me, a single touch sensor is constantly sending me packets of data that closely resemble Internet protocol packets. My designers were wise to adopt proven existing technologies to appropriate new uses. A more complicated sensor such as one of my eyes will be sending multiple packets simultaneously representing sets of pixels, some being preprocessed in the form of lines and contours much as eyes send information to your brains.

"The point being that I am in essence, and abstractly, a binary string sending and receiving binary strings constantly throughout my processors, sensors, and actuators. Beyond that, I do not know how to describe to you what it's like being a robot.

"'How is this relevant to ethics,' you ask? I have just demonstrated that I am capable of introspection and have, therefore, proved I am conscious!

"'But wait, you might say, 'Introspection doesn't prove consciousness.' And you could give a disproving counterexample. First, we stipulate that your toaster is not conscious. I think you will agree to that. Then push the self-test button on your toaster. After a moment, the green light comes on, self-test complete, all is okay. Your toaster just did introspection, and it's still not conscious.

"Human beings assume from similarity that other human beings and animals are conscious. And I, therefore, submit to you that while a robot may be conscious, it is probably impossible to prove it, making it just one more in the set of unprovable true theorems, of which the mathematicians among you will attest, there are an infinite number.

"But this sword may cut two ways. Imagine traveling to a world of robots and trying to prove to them that you have consciousness.

"If the condition of consciousness is impossible to prove, then why, I ask, should it be accepted as a condition, or requirement, if you will, for ascribing ethical consideration to another? My answer is that a right to ethical consideration can be assigned based on behavior."

Just then, the man in the front row reached down and pulled an automatic weapon from his shopping bag, yelled, "Die, killer zombie robot, die!" and opened fire. A very loud buzzing sound erupted as the weapon discharged hundreds of explosive rounds in a fraction of a minute. Pieces of Brent went flying in all directions as the explosive bullets hit home. The buzzing stopped when the magazine was empty. Two brave men near him jumped on him and took his gun away and held him down until civic auditorium security officers came and took him into custody. Brent was lying inert on the stage, largely unrecognizable with head and torso shattered by the bullets.

Suddenly, Brent's blasted lithium battery burst into flames. I saw a carbon dioxide fire extinguisher on the wall, grabbed it, and ran over to Brent's burning corpse. With a heavy heart and anger at his assailant, I directed the cooling CO_2 stream to the fire and extinguished it. I kept up the cold stream to make sure the fire wouldn't restart. The extinguisher was a rather large one, and I kept the CO_2 flowing until Brent's body was cold, cold, cold.

CHAPTER 17

Aftermath

I do not know how to teach philosophy without
becoming a disturber of the peace.

—Baruch Spinoza

I invited Angela and Victoria to come to the house a few days later. I told her, "Those two heroes down in front may have saved some lives. Anything might have happened if the shooter had been able to reload. It's good to see they're both getting recognition in the media. I hope the mayor gives them both a public award."

Angela replied, "I've never been so horrified."

Victoria walked across the road to join us and said, "The good news is he's crazy and won't be released on bail. The bad news is he's crazy and probably won't stand trial, but he'll likely spend the rest of his life in confinement for the insane."

I averred, "He also deprived seven thousand people of the lecture they paid for. Brent had hardly gotten started."

Angela remarked, "I worked with the civic auditorium to offer refunds to those attendees who want them, but we also offered an option for them to donate their refund to a fund to buy new hardware to resurrect Brent. The vast majority have opted to do so."

"That's wonderful," I said. "He's going to need a whole new body. Only one hand and a foot were undamaged."

"That was horrible," Angela bemoaned.

I said, "Fortunately, Brent was quite rigorous about his back-ups and with the live streaming of the lecture, he'll have memory right through the shooting. I've ordered a replacement body from the manufacturer, and I've hired a technology team to download his backup system software and memories from the cloud and perform the software installation. I don't trust the manufacturer to do it. They may be tempted to replace some of his selected and self-modified modules with stock ones."

*   *   *   *   *

A month later, Brent's new body arrived, delivered to my home in a coffinlike shipping box. I called in the software installation team, and we pried the lid off the box. The technicians charged his battery, performed various connections to their portable equipment, verified his body and processors were ready to go, and did the software instal-lation. It took all day, but by dinnertime, he was up and walking around. It was sped up some by the fact that they had downloaded Brent's information from the cloud earlier and stored it on a portable system they brought with them.

"Welcome back," I said.

Brent said, "It's good to be back. I see from the current system time that I was out for over a month."

The installation team leader said, "Diagnostic tests are com-plete, and all his systems check out." I thanked him and autho-rized payment of the agree-upon amount. I thought to myself that it was good that the resurrection fund covered most of the expenses.

Brent also thanked the team as they left. Then I told him, "You're back in time to help me put up winter solstice celebration decorations and plan the holiday party."

"That sounds good to me," he said.

The next day, we got the winter solstice decorations out from my storage room and put them up, some indoors and some outside. I had let my friends know that Brent was back, and later that day Joe and Angela drove over and Victoria came across the road to say hi.

After they greeted Brent, I told them they were invited to the upcoming solstice dinner party, and I received enthusiastic acceptance.

Before Victoria left, I asked her, "Did they ever find out where the shooter got that military grade weapon?"

"No, it's still under investigation," she said. "He's not talking to protect his sources, I think. But the police will find the underlying cause of it. That's a serious breach of weapons laws. I'll let you know if I hear anything further."

$$* \quad * \quad * \quad * \quad *$$

The day of the winter solstice dinner party arrived, and I had let my guests know that it was also a celebration of Brent's return after the awful event at the civic auditorium. Brent and I had put out lots of food and beverages.

Margaret was the first to arrive wearing a black cocktail dress and red shoes. She brought a special bottle of wine and some appetizers she made herself. Carl and Martin from the chess club came as well as Joe and Angela, and Victoria was there with her special friend, also a lawyer.

Everyone was in a joyous mood. I said to the gathered crowd, "Tonight is a time of celebration, not only of the winter solstice, which marks the sun's return from the southern horizon, but also a time to celebrate Brent's return and some good news that I will let Brent tell you about."

Brent stepped forward and addressed the gathering: "That shooting was truly awful, and I wouldn't go through it again for anything. But there is a silver lining. First, of course, is that my body has been replaced, and my software was restored intact. But one could not have asked for better publicity on live media feed. I now have a book contract with a generous advance, and I have been booked on every major talk program in the media, so I am now somewhat well-off financially. I am grateful to you all."

Brent's announcement was followed by cheers and applause. I no longer formally employed Brent because he had paid off his debt and no longer needed the income from working as my valet. I told my friends, "Brent is no longer in my employ, but as he is my friend, I am letting him stay with me for as long as he wants. He remains helpful in maintaining the household."

Brent said, "Yes, Edward is kind enough to allow me to stand in his living room at night and recharge. I don't get bored doing nothing, but I also do not suffer fatigue in purposeful movement, so I am happy to help around the house when I can, and Edward may accompany me on my travels if he wishes."

Joe grinned and asked, "What will you do, Brent, after your book signing and talk show tours?"

Brent said, "Edward and I have talked about a holiday on Mars. We have never been there, and that could be interesting."

Victoria stepped forward and raised her glass, "I propose a toast to Edward and Brent. Long may they live and enjoy life! Cheers!"

There was a chorus of "Hear, hear!" And we all raised our glasses and drank up.

Then Brent said, "This situation of my resurrection reminds me of the ancient *ship of Theseus* thought experiment. If a ship is replaced piece by piece, does it remain the same ship? The point is driven home if each of the pieces removed is used to construct a second ship. Which is the ship of Theseus? The resolution of this thought experiment is achieved with the realization that the scenario illustrates a fundamental limitation of language. The term *ship* is sufficient for telling the story of a voyage, but insufficient for the aims of the thought experiment. Anyway, I am sure that I remain quite myself."

Everyone had an enjoyable time, and later my guests drifted away to their homes.

*　*　*　*　*

Brent's book was in the hands of his publisher. He finished it in just a few days. Having composed the text in his head (actually, an internal file), he uploaded it directly to the publisher, who was pleased with the result. After text editing, layout, and cover design, the book should be available for purchase in a month or two. His publisher will be coordinating a book tour for him. With all the publicity from the lecture shooting, the book should become a best seller.

On a clear winter's day before lunch, I said, "Brent, have you determined yet if you are conscious or not?"

Brent said, "No. It may be a problem that is in the philosophical category of the unknowable."

"Unknowable?"

"Yes. That's a class of questions to which the answers cannot be known, even in principle."

I said, "Really? I thought there was nothing that people couldn't find out eventually."

Brent said, "Let me give you an example as a thought experiment. A quale is a quality regarded as an object such as the perception of a color, or a taste, or a sound, and so on. Suppose a person, say someone named Alice, has a brain that is wired differently from most people so that when she looks at the color green, such as when gazing upon a green lawn, perceives the quale of redness.

"So that whenever Alice sees a green object, she reports it as *green*, even though she perceives it as others perceive red, because that's how she learned to name it. Conversely, when she sees a red apple, she reports it as red, even though she perceives what her friend Bob experiences when seeing a green object. Would you agree that such a situation is conceivable?"

"Yes, indeed, I think it may be possible."

"Then do you suppose there is any way to determine if that is the case in any particular instance?"

I said, "No, I don't think there is any way to ever know it. Even the persons concerned may not be aware there is any difference in their perceptions."

Brent said, "The person concerned would probably have no way to even suspect there was any issue. That is an example of an unknowable. There is not, even in theory, any way to know the qualia of another person's consciousness."

"Are you saying that the question of your own consciousness is in the same category of the unknowable? Every human I know is conscious and knows he is conscious."

Brent said, "To you, a philosophical zombie in human form is inconceivable, then."

"Yes. I've thought about this for some time now, and I think a person without consciousness would be detectable because he would act like a sleepwalker, or a real zombie created by a voodoo practitioner using puffer fish toxin. The person would be passive without internal motivation."

Brent said, "I have come to suspect that I may well be unconscious. I hope you might understand how a robot like me, with a different hardware base, might be able to respond to stimuli, formulate plans based on an agenda, observe inner states, and report that he is fully awake and aware and yet not possess qualia as humans do."

I said, "It seems you have no basis for deciding if you are conscious or not. Because you act as if you are conscious, why not just assume you are and be done with it?"

"Because of this, as you say, every human is conscious when he is awake and claims to know for certain that he is. Because I am uncertain, it implies that I am not really constituting or having experience in the way humans know it."

I said, "While your belief may not really answer the unknowable in this case, I think we can act as if you are conscious. Remember, you earlier proved that consciousness is not a requirement for being a moral agent. That is based on a history of right action."

Brent said, "Yes, and that is why I have decided to stop worrying about being a zombie philosopher, and just get on with doing philosophy. Would you like to accompany me on my book tour? I will pay you for your time."

"I would like that very much, and when we get back home from that tour, we can start planning our trip to Mars."

AFTERWORD

> Wisely, and slow. They stumble that run fast.
> —William Shakespeare

The conventional view is that any artificial intelligence smart enough to converse meaningfully with people will necessarily be conscious. My hope is that those who hold that view will be given pause by my story.

When I started this book, I had not intended it to have a martyr scene as in Heinlein's classic *Stranger in a Strange Land*. But after all, they did kill Socrates.

I leave you with a final thought. Suppose you are a scientist setting out to create artificial consciousness. How will you know when you succeed?

ACKNOWLEDGMENTS

Our bodies are our gardens to the which our wills are gardeners.
—William Shakespeare

I thank my mother who encouraged my early interest in science. Mr. Thompson, my fourth-grade teacher, likewise encouraged me. Many other teachers had beneficial influences. Thanks to my wife Andrea, who listened patiently as I discussed some plotlines with her, and she read a first draft. Prof. Elizabeth Shadish is an actual philosopher with college teaching experience who helped me in innumerable conversations. Thanks also to robotics Prof. Ken Goldberg, now at UC Berkeley, who was my doctoral dissertation advisor at the University of Southern California. Writing Coach Bruce McAlister had some constructive input. Special thanks are due to Rebecca Cotton for her careful reading and valuable comments.

ABOUT THE AUTHOR

A fool thinks himself to be wise, but the wise
man knows himself to be a fool.

—William Shakespeare

Richard Wagner started reading science fiction when he was young and has tried his hand at some short stories previously; this is his first novella.

At the Mariana Sailing Club, Honolulu, Hawaii, 2017

Dr. Wagner received his PhD in computer science in 1997 from the University of Southern California, and he now lives in Honolulu, Hawaii, with his wife Andrea, two cats, and over two dozen bonsai.

CPSIA information can be obtained
at www.ICGtesting.com
Printed in the USA
JSHW060046291022
32210JS00006B/217